Geronimo Stilton

Ebenezer Scrooge

Bob Cratchit

Tim Cratchit

Belle

Marley

Ghost of Christmas Future

Ghost of Christmas Past

Ghost of Christmas Present

A Christmas Carol

Dear rodent readers,

My love for great stories began a long time ago, when I was still a young mouselet. I spent hours and hours reading wonderful books! They took me on fantastic adventures to mysterious, faraway lands. Reading made my imagination soar — and it made me want to become a writer, too!

So I thought I'd share with you a great

literary mousterpiece. Ebenezer Scrooge is a stingy, grouchy old mouse whose favorite pastime is making money. He can't understand why anyone would take time off from work to celebrate Christmas. But one Christmas Eve, Scrooge has some unbelievable encounters that just might change his mind. It's a story you'll never forget!

Geronimo Stilton

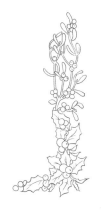

Published by Scholastic Inc., *Publishers since 1920*, 557 Broadway, New York, NY 10012. SCHOLASTIC and associated logos are trademarks and/ or registered trademarks of Scholastic Inc.

Stilton is the name of a famous English cheese. It is a registered trademark of the Stilton Cheese Makers' Association. For more information, go to stiltoncheese.com.

ISBN 978-1-338-54695-8

Original text by Charles Dickens
Adapted by Geronimo Stilton
Original Italian title *Canto di Natale*
Cover by Flavio Ferron
Illustrations by Andrea Denegri and Edwyn Nori
Graphics by Silvia Bovo

Special thanks to AnnMarie Anderson
Translated by Emily Clement
Interior design by Kevin Callahan/BNGO Books

Printed in China 62
First edition, October 2019

Geronimo Stilton

A Christmas Carol

Based on the novel
by Charles Dickens

Scholastic Inc.

Part One

Ebenezer Scrooge

There was no doubt about it: Jacob Marley had passed on to a better place. The documents had been signed by the doctor, his assistant, the funeral director, and by Ebenezer Scrooge.

When Scrooge signed something, that made it official. Scrooge had been Marley's business partner, the executor of his will, and the mouse's only heir.

Now, you might be thinking Scrooge was feeling *sad* about the loss of his business partner. But Marley had been quite old, and he had been sick. So, while Scrooge certainly wasn't happy to be attending a funeral, he had more important things on his mind, such as his business.

You might be surprised by this coldness, but for Ebenezer Scrooge, business came before everything and everymouse.

The first business decision Scrooge made after Marley's death related to the sign outside his office. It read, **Scrooge & Marley**, and Scrooge decided it would stay that way.

But it wasn't out of respect for the memory of his lost FRIEND. No, it was because the business was known by that name. Scrooge might lose money if he changed the company's name and his clients didn't recognize the business.

The one thing Scrooge LOVED more than anything else was MONEY. No one in London knew more about scrimping to save a penny than that old cheapskate mouse. His heart was as hard as steel, and he was as miserly, crabby, and closed-up as an oyster trying to keep its precious pearl to itself.

The chill inside Scrooge **froze** his snout into a scowl, made his lips pucker into a pout, and sharpened his already-pointy nose. His head and eyebrows were covered in hairs as white as a layer of frost, and his whiskers and beard were as prickly as a row of icicles.

Scrooge managed to spread a chill everywhere he went, even in a room warmed by a crackling fire. Everyone who approached him felt it and took a step back, **shivering** and pulling their sweaters tightly around them.

Inside Scrooge's office, it was the **WORST**. Since Scrooge spent every hour of every day there (even holidays), it was practically a

FREEZER! That's because Scrooge was too cheap to spend any of his money on heating coals to warm the room.

Out on the street, it was the same—no one stopped Scrooge to say **HELLO**, not even so much as to wave his way. Beggars never asked him for a single cent. They seemed to know he would never, ever part with a single dime! Even dogs tugged at their leashes and *dragged* their owners away when they saw Scrooge coming.

But did Ebenezer Scrooge care? No, not at all! He was perfectly content to be left alone in his office, where he spent hours COUNTING and **DOUBLE-COUNTING** his gold. In fact, he preferred it this way.

Seven years passed after the death of Scrooge's business partner, Jacob Marley. They were seven lonely years, but Scrooge

didn't mind as long as his piles of gold continued to grow.

Life for Scrooge was very simple, until one cold December, when something very **UNEXPECTED** happened . . .

Bah, Humbug!

It was the most wonderful day of the year, **Christmas Eve**. Scrooge was working in his office. It was terribly cold, and outside the air was crisp and the street was thick with fog.

Mice were rushing along the road, clapping their paws together to keep them warm and stamping their boots on the ground to keep them from **FREEZING**.

The town clock had struck three in the afternoon, but it was already **D A R K** outside. Inside buildings and homes around London, candles flickered, but the fog seemed to slip in through every crack and keyhole.

It was as if the fog didn't want to stay out

in the cold and couldn't wait to warm up in front of a nice warm FIREPLACE!

The door to Scrooge's office was open so that he could keep an EYE on his sole employee, Bob Cratchit. Young Cratchit was working in the front room, which was really more of a closet. It was a real hole in the wall!

At that moment, poor Bob Cratchit was busy copying some letters. The fire in the hearth was barely an ember, and Cratchit had a big white scarf wrapped around his neck in an attempt to keep himself from FREEZING. He had to stop writing from time to time to **blow** on his paws to warm them.

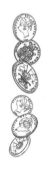

Scrooge's assistant knew better than to use more than one or two pieces of coal

in the stove, and he only added extra fuel to the **FIRE** when his fur was almost frozen. Scrooge always took advantage of him, but Cratchit never complained.

It was partly because Cratchit was poor and needed the job, and partly because he had a kind and gentle nature. Bob Cratchit was a truly **GOOD SOUL**!

"Merry Christmas, Uncle!" a **HAPPY** voice shouted from the entryway.

A tall, stout young mouse came into the room. His eyes were bright, his cheeks **red**, and his smile warm enough to cheer anyone up. Well, anyone except Scrooge, that is.

"Bah, humbug!" Scrooge muttered.

"Humbug, Uncle?" his nephew replied.

"Aren't you happy it's Christmas Eve?"

Scrooge sneered again, and his **thick** eyebrows united across his forehead.

"Happy, happy . . . bah!" squeaked Scrooge. "What right do you have to be *happy*, as poor as you are? Aren't you poor enough to be **SAD**?"

His nephew, who was named Fred, just smiled.

"Come, come, Uncle, what about you?" he replied. "What right do you have to be **ANGRY**? Aren't you rich enough to be happy?"

"Rich? Me? *Rich?!*" Scrooge replied, scandalized. "What do you mean, **RICH**? I may have money, but I also have too much to do! It's especially *bad* at Christmas, when the year is ending. I have so much work to do squaring away the accounts. Christmas isn't

a happy time . . . it's just another **hassle**!"

"Okay, okay," his nephew gave in. "I won't change your mind. But I do want to **CELEBRATE**. Uncle, I came here to invite you to lunch tomorrow at our house, seeing as you're always **ALONE** on Christmas. Will you come?"

"Lunch? On Christmas Day?!" Scrooge gasped. "Bah, humbug! I can't get away."

"Okay," Fred said with a shrug. "Happy holidays, anyway, dear Uncle. And don't work too much!"

With that, Fred closed the door and disappeared into the fog. The office quickly seemed even **COLDER** and darker than before.

A Simple Request

Scrooge went back to his work, grumbling. He was so busy he didn't realize Bob Cratchit had just let two *gentlemice* into the office. Scrooge noticed them only when they were right in front of him. He eyed them warily, as if they were two criminals who had just escaped from prison.

"Um, good day, Mr. Marley," the first mouse greeted him **warmly**. "You're Marley of 'Scrooge and Marley,' correct?"

"Marley has been dead for seven years," Scrooge corrected the mouse grumpily. "He died on this very day: Christmas Eve."

The gentlemice blushed and exchanged a nervous **LOOK**.

"Um, my apologies," the first mouse replied.

"Then you must be Mr. Scrooge," the second mouse jumped in. "Surely your generosity must be equal to that of the dearly departed partner, Mr. Marley."

At the word "generosity," Scrooge's eyes widened, and he flinched as if he had been stuck by a pin.

"Since it *is* **Christmas**, Mr. Scrooge, it's always good to think of the needy," the first mouse went on, turning over his hat in his paws.

"Yes, the poor, the sick, the homeless . . ." the second mouse chimed in.

Scrooge raised an eyebrow. "Tell me, gentlemice, are there still **SHELTERS** in this town?"

"U-um, yes, of course th-there are, but . . ." STUTTERED the first mouse.

"And are there hospitals? And nursing homes?" Scrooge pressed on.

"Why, yes, there are many!" the second mouse exclaimed in surprise.

Scrooge gave one of his rare smiles. "Oh, wonderful, then! I was AFRAID I'd have to donate money from my own pocket in order to cover the expenses of the poor, the sick, and the homeless. But I am so pleased that London's civic institutions are still functioning *perfectly*. Now, if you will excuse me, gentlemice, I have work to do. **GOOD DAY.**"

The two mice quickly found themselves back out in the cold, SQUEAKLESS.

No Handouts!

heered by the fact that he had ended the conversation without shelling out a single CENT, Scrooge went back to work.

Outside, the **DARKNESS** grew even deeper. The fog was so thick it seemed you could cut it like a knife through soft cheese. The carriages moved down the street at a SNaiL'S pace, and the cold was so intense it seemed to bite one's cheeks.

Inside Scrooge's office, it was finally closing time. This was always a sad time of the day for Scrooge, as he knew he wouldn't have anything to do at home.

Bob Cratchit, on the other paw, couldn't wait to get home. He knew his family was waiting for him so they could begin their

Christmas Eve supper. Cratchit snuffed out his candle and *raced* to put on his cap. Then he wrapped his white scarf more tightly around his neck, as he couldn't **afford** an overcoat.

Scrooge spotted him out of the corner of his eye and scowled.

"Hmph!" he grumbled. "I imagine tomorrow you'll want to stay home all day, Cratchit."

The poor mouse BLUSHED. "Oh, well . . . actually yes, sir," he squeaked. "It *is* Christmas, after all."

"You don't need to remind me!" the old mouse growled. "What could you have to **CELEBRATE**, when you earn so little and have a family to take care of?"

But Bob Cratchit just smiled.

"Don't say that, Mr. Scrooge," he replied.

"I have plenty to CeLeBRate. And it's just one day at home . . ."

"Well, you'd better be here at DAWN the next day," Scrooge snapped. "And you'll be docked pay, understand?! There are NO HANDOUTS here at Scrooge and Marley!"

Bob Cratchit agreed, then raced out the office door in the blink of an eye. He hurried down the street, his big white scarf WAVING in the fog like a flag. He couldn't wait to get home to play with his children and celebrate a joyful Christmas Eve!

Marley's Ghost

By the time Scrooge turned onto his own street, the **L I G H T S** from the shops were already out. He noticed the signs up and down the street were decorated with branches of **GREEN HOLLY** and **red berries**.

"Lights, colors, decorations . . . bah!" Scrooge muttered, shaking his head in dismay. "What a waste!"

A sweet-looking mouselet stood on the corner, singing Christmas carols and holding out a basket for **coins**. Scrooge passed by, ignoring him.

Scrooge shuffled along slowly, leaning on his walking stick and taking care not to **slip** on the icy street.

He stopped to eat dinner at his usual shabby tavern, and after reading all the newspapers, he finally headed home.

To save money on rent, Scrooge lived in the house that had belonged to his partner, Jacob Marley. The dark, cold rooms were so gloomy no one would have wanted to live there. No one except Scrooge, that is. The old mouse knew the way there like the back of his paw, but that evening the fog was *thicker* than usual. It took some EFFORT for Scrooge to find his own front door.

When Scrooge finally made it home, he looked up at the front door in astonishment. The door knocker had suddenly turned into . . . a snout?! How could that be? Scrooge **rubbed** his eyes in disbelief.

It wasn't just an *illusion*. The door

knocker definitely was a snout: Jacob Marley's snout, to be precise!

It stared at Scrooge, wide-eyed, its fiery red hair FLOATING above it as if it had been ruffled by a breath of warm air. As Scrooge stared in disbelief, Marley's snout vanished as quickly as it had appeared.

Disturbed, the old mouse rushed to turn the key in the lock. Scrooge stepped inside, his heart beating in his ears and his head spinning. He quickly shut the door behind him, double-checking that it was LOCKED.

Scrooge took a deep breath. He had to calm down. He lit the candles in the entryway and began to climb the stairs slowly, taking them one by one. At one point he almost lost his balance, and the candlestick dripped wax on his foot, burning his paw.

"**OUCh!**" Scrooge cried out in surprise.

His legs trembled as he checked every room in the house. The sitting room, the bedroom, the closet . . . everything seemed to be in its place.

What nonsense! Scrooge thought. *I must be seeing things. There's nothing to be afraid of!*

He put on his **nightshirt**, sleeping cap, and slippers and settled into his armchair in front of the tiny and not-very-warm FIRE.

He had barely rested his head on the back of the chair when he realized that the bell—which had been used to call the servants in former days—was ringing softly. Scrooge jumped up in surprise as the bell got louder and louder, and then stopped abruptly. A second later, he heard another sound—a deep metallic **clanging**, as if someone was dragging a heavy chain up the stairs.

Scrooge gulped. Could it be a **ghost**?

No, of course not! Scrooge thought. *Ghosts don't exist!*

Yet the sound grew even **LOUDER** until it was just a few steps away.

BANG!

The bedroom door *flew* open! For the second time that evening, Scrooge found himself snout-to-snout with Jacob Marley. This time, though, it wasn't just a vision. It was a real ghost.

Why Are You in Chains?

Scrooge took in the familiar snout, the **waistcoat**, the stockings, and the shoes: it really was Marley! His body was so transparent that Scrooge could see right through him to the pair of buttons that decorated the back of his jacket.

Marley was wrapped up in a long, heavy chain that wound around his body like a steel snake with a tail. But it wasn't a normal chain. Padlocks, chests, keys, and account books all dangled from the chain, dragging Marley down. They were all items the businessmouse had used frequently when he was **ALIVE**.

Scrooge couldn't believe his **EYES**.

"What do you want from me?" he asked the ghost, trying not to be too rude.

"Ah, many things!" was the reply. It was even Marley's voice!

"Wh-who are you?" Scrooge stuttered, cold sweat dripping from his brow.

"Who *was I*, you mean," the ghost corrected him. "Don't you recognize me? We were partners for years. It's me, Jacob Marley!"

"Can you . . . can you sit down?" Scrooge asked.

"I can," the ghost replied. And he settled his transparent body into the chair facing Scrooge.

The fur, the tails of his jacket, and the ribbons on the ghost's clothing were

constantly *moving*, as if a gentle breeze were blowing all around him.

"You don't believe I'm here, do you?" he asked.

Scrooge shrugged. "Why should I? Surely you're just in my **IMAGINATION**!"

Actually, Scrooge had no idea what to think. He was terrified, but he was trying his best to remain **calm**. The sound of the ghost's voice was enough to scare the fur off his tail!

"Why are you all chained up?" Scrooge asked, staring at the strange chain with horror and curiosity.

"I built this chain myself, throughout my life," Marley's ghost explained, a **sad** look on his snout. "I welded it ring by ring, piece by piece. Now all it does is **weigh** me down. Do you want to see it up close?"

Scrooge trembled fearfully.

"Or maybe you're curious about your own chain," the ghost continued. "I can tell you that, when I died seven years ago, your chain was already as long and HEAVY as mine is now. But since then you've worked hard to make yourself even richer, right?"

Scrooge looked around in alarm, as if he expected to see fifty or sixty feet of iron and padlocks wrapped around his tail. But there was nothing there.

"Jacob, please give me some WORDS of comfort," Scrooge begged. "You're SCARING me!"

The ghost shook his head. "I'm sorry, Ebenezer, but that's not possible. I'm not in a position to comfort anyone. In fact, I can't stay much longer. I have to get back to the office. My heart has always been

chained to work, and so that's where I must stay for all eternity!"

With that, Marley's ghost cried out, shaking his chains and wringing his paws. He seemed so distraught that Scrooge felt his heart ache for his old friend.

"Why do you suffer so?" Scrooge asked. "You were such a **GREAT** businessmouse! Why aren't you a satisfied ghost?"

"Business!" Marley's ghost repeated, raising his eyes to the sky. "That's the problem! Friends, affection, family: these should have been my *business*. My dealings were but a drop of water in the ocean of truly important things! Oh, if only I had been less **SELFISH** . . ."

He lifted the chains, as if they were the cause of all his **PAIN**, and then dropped them to the ground again sadly.

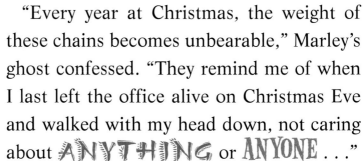

"Every year at Christmas, the weight of these chains becomes unbearable," Marley's ghost confessed. "They remind me of when I last left the office alive on Christmas Eve and walked with my head down, not caring about ANYTHING or ANYONE . . ."

Scrooge saw himself closing the office door earlier that evening and felt a deep sense of **regret**.

"But you still have a chance!" the ghost said. "Tonight, you will be visited by three ghosts."

Scrooge's hopes crumbled. Three ghosts! "Is this my only hope?!" he replied.

"The first will arrive at one o'clock," Marley's ghost continued. "The rest will follow. Pay attention, Scrooge! Listen to what they tell you. And now, if you will excuse me, I must go."

Marley's ghost rose from the chair, floated over to the window, and pulled it open. An icy chill invaded the room. Curious, Scrooge walked over and saw an impressive sight: a stream of ghosts FLOATED by outside!

One old, one young, one tall, and one short. They were all as transparent as the air around them.

Marley's ghost slipped in among them and drifted off into the NIGHT.

"Remember what I told you, Scrooge!" he called out. "Remember!"

Then the parade of ghosts disappeared, swallowed up by the fog.

Scrooge closed the window and hugged his arms around his chest. He was CONFUSED, shocked, and exhausted. Unsure of what else to do, he put out his candle, climbed into his bed, and fell asleep.

Part Two

Bong, Bong, Bong . . .

When Scrooge woke up, the room was **DARK**.

The old mouse squinted. Where was he? Oh, yes, he was asleep in bed. The memory of Marley's ghost hit him like a LIGHTNING bolt, and Scrooge sat straight up immediately, listening for the slightest noise.

Bong, bong, bong . . .

The clock chimed twelve times.

Scrooge jumped. It was already midnight!

He got out of bed and began to pace the room nervously without knowing why. Then he found himself at the window, peering out into the cold, dark night. The fog was so **thick** Scrooge could barely see a thing, but he could tell that the street was

deserted, and all the lights were out. Scrooge could feel the chill of the night **deep** in his bones.

The clock sounded twelve thirty. Scrooge SUDDENLY remembered what Marley's ghost had told him: at one o'clock, the first ghost would visit him.

Alarmed, Scrooge got back in bed and waited. Twenty minutes to go . . . then ten . . . then five . . .

BONG!

"It's one o'clock!" cried Scrooge as he leaped out of bed.

Scrooge was just about to laugh with relief that nothing had happened, when the bed curtains parted, and a small, pale hand appeared. Scrooge **gasped**, his heart in his throat as the curtains opened all the way.

The ghost appeared. She looked like a

child, but with long white hair that fell down around her shoulders. She wore a pale tunic decorated with flowers, and she had a shiny belt tied around her waist. Although the clothing was very light, the ghost didn't seem to feel the cold. But the most surprising thing about the ghost was her strange head covering, which resembled a candle snuffer, and the bright ray of light that radiated all around her.

"Wh-who are you?" Scrooge stuttered, awestruck by the dazzling vision.

"I am the Ghost of Christmas Past," she replied. Her voice was sweet and so soft it sounded as if she were very far away.

"And why are you here?" the old mouse asked.

The ghost gently GRABBED Scrooge by the arm.

"I'm here for your happiness," she replied with a smile. Then she led him to the window.

"Don't make me go out there!" Scrooge squeaked, suddenly **afraid**. "It's cold and dark, and I'm only in a nightshirt. I might fall!"

"Shhhhh," the ghost shushed him. "You won't fall. You just need to rely on *this*."

She took his paw and placed it over his heart. Then she squeezed it *softly*, and together, they passed right through the wall.

Do You Remember, Scrooge?

Scrooge couldn't believe his eyes.

"Oh my!" he cried, *astounded*.

Logically, he knew that the city street full of shops and homes was on the other side of the wall. But instead, Scrooge found himself in the **snow-covered** countryside. And it wasn't just any landscape, either; it was a place he knew well.

"I **grew up** here!" he shouted. "I was a mouselet here!"

"Do you recognize this road?" the Ghost of Christmas Past asked.

Scrooge looked around him. "Do I **recognize** it?!" he asked. "Why, I'd know it with my eyes shut!"

The ghost gave him a **SAD** look. "How strange that until just now you seem to have forgotten it," she remarked.

Scrooge blushed with SHAME. It was true. He hadn't thought about his youth in so long that it almost seemed to belong to someone else!

As they walked along, the old mouse recognized every hedge, tree, and gate. He even recalled all of the bends in the river and the **PICKET FENCES**! They reached an old schoolhouse and saw several mouselets streaming out the front door. But none of them noticed Scrooge and the ghost.

"They're just **shadows**," the ghost explained. "They may seem real to you, but they are ghosts, like me."

"**NO!**" Scrooge squeaked, looking over the little STUDENTS. "I know them all!"

Tears suddenly clouded his vision, and a wave of memories washed over him.

"Merry Christmas! Merry Christmas!" the mouselets squeaked happily to one another before they rushed home.

Only one mouse remained in the classroom. Scrooge recognized himself instantly.

Little Ebenezer was intently studying mathematics. He seemed so sad and lonely in that empty classroom that the old mouse felt his heart ache for his younger self.

"I remember staying and studying after everyone else had left," he murmured. "I never went out to play with my CLASSMATES because it seemed like such a waste of time."

A tear ran down his wrinkled snout.

Embarrassed, he quickly brushed it away.

The Ghost of Christmas Past watched him *closely*.

"What are you thinking about?" she asked.

Scrooge bowed his head. "I'm thinking about a little mouse who was singing along my street tonight. I avoided him so I wouldn't have to give him money. But now I wish I had stopped to **LISTEN** and give him a dime."

The ghost **SMiLED**.

"It's too late for that, I'm afraid," she said softly. "But let's go on! We have another Christmas to see."

It's Christmas, Brother!

s soon as the Ghost of Christmas Past spoke, little Scrooge began to change right in front of Scrooge's eyes. He **grew** and **grew** until he looked more like a young mouse than a mouselet. Even though he had changed, the classroom was still the same, though now the paint on the walls was *peeling* a bit more than before.

Young Scrooge was no longer seated at his desk. Instead he was walking back and forth, as if **preoccupied**.

Suddenly, someone threw the classroom door open.

A happy mouselet in a pretty blue dress dashed in like a little **tornado**. As soon as she saw young Scrooge, she THREW her arms around his neck and covered his snout in kisses.

"Brother, Brother!" she squealed happily. "It's Christmas! What are you doing here? It's time to come home!"

"You're right, little Fan," young Scrooge said tenderly. "I've studied enough for today."

Then he hugged his little sister, and she snuggled her head into his neck and laughed contentedly.

Old Scrooge couldn't hold back an affectionate smile.

"Dear little Fan . . ."

"She was truly kind, wasn't she?" the ghost asked. "And she had such a big heart!"

"Yes, she was a *wonderful* mouse . . ." Scrooge agreed, moved by the ghost's kind words. "But she's no longer with us."

"She had a family, though, didn't she?" asked the ghost.

"J-just my nephew," the old mouse **StutteReD** awkwardly. "He came to see me this morning, but . . ."

Scrooge trailed off as he recalled how he had treated Fred. He had been so cold and unpleasant to his dear nephew. After all, Fred was his only family! Why hadn't he EMBRACED him, as Fan had done to him when he was a young mouse?

Scrooge stuffed his paws in the pockets of his nightshirt, lost in thought. His heart was **heavy**, and he felt very TIRED.

Enough Work, Time to Celebrate!

Scrooge was lost in his thoughts when he realized the landscape had changed yet again. The school and countryside had become a **busy** city street. Passersby rushed around, carrying boxes and bags, while carriages dug long, **DEEP** tracks in the snow. It was Christmas Eve, and the streets were brightly lit and decorated with sweet-smelling wreaths tied with red ribbons.

The Ghost of Christmas Past brought Scrooge to the **door** of a shop.

"Do you recognize it?" she asked him.

"How could I not?!" Scrooge replied instantly. "I worked here as an apprentice. It was my first **JOB**!"

The moment he crossed the threshold, Scrooge saw an **old** gentlemouse in a wig seated at a desk so high that his fur brushed the ceiling.

"My word, that's old Fezziwig!" he squeaked EXCITEDLY.

Fezziwig put down his pen and consulted the time: it was seven o'clock. He rubbed his paws together eagerly and called out, "Ebenezer! Dick! Come!"

A twenty-year-old Scrooge and another young mouse of about the same age entered the room.

"And that's Dick Wilkins!" shouted Scrooge, even though NO ONE could hear him.

"**Huzzah**, youngsters!" cried the merry Fezziwig. "Enough work, it's Christmas

Eve! Come on, close your books and let's get ready for the PARTY!

"Let's clear away these ledgers and papers and sweep the floor—quickly!" Fezziwig encouraged them, **spinning** from one side of the room to the other like a dancer. "The guests will be here soon!"

An hour later, a fiddler knocked on the door.

"May I?" he asked politely.

"Why, of course, come in, come in!" Fezziwig greeted him **warmly**. "Make yourself comfortable over there. A bit of MUSIC is just what we need!"

They were quickly joined by dozens of guests. Everyone was eager to warm their paws by the fire and catch up with old friends. There were drinks and delicious food,

followed by the most **delectable** sweets.

Everyone brought something to share, and everyone got a taste of something on this joyous occasion.

When the music began, the guests broke into couples and began to **SPIN** around the shop as if they were in a ballroom. No one knew the steps, and everyone stepped on someone else's paws. But instead of complaining, the mice just laughed and continued to waltz around *happily*.

When the clock struck eleven, the guests went home, exhausted and happy.

What's Wrong, Scrooge?

As he watched the party unfold around him, old Scrooge STARED at the scene, his eyes wide. It was all exactly as it had happened in his past! The happiness, the friendships, the *excitement* . . .

Scrooge had a strong urge to run around and HUG everyone, shouting, "I remember you! Oh, what WONDERFUL times we had together!"

But he didn't do it. He was too old and hardened by life to let his emotions run free.

"What's wrong?" the Ghost of Christmas past asked.

Scrooge couldn't answer.

"That Fezziwig was a real **lazy mouse**, wasn't he?" the ghost continued, shaking her head. "He should have been working hard, but instead he was celebrating . . ."

"But it was Christmas Eve!" Scrooge replied. "And he was a WONDERFUL boss. He was always so kind and generous. The pay wasn't much, but he always treated us well —"

He STOPPED suddenly.

"What is it?" asked the ghost.

Scrooge put his paws in his pockets and hung his head.

"Oh, it's nothing really," the old mouse mumbled. "It's just that maybe I should have been kinder to my employee, Bob Cratchit, last night. I didn't even wish him a merry Christmas."

The ghost gave him a small smile. "Oh, but

that's all **NONSENSE**, isn't it?"

"Nonsense?" repeated old Scrooge, ashamed. "I did say that, didn't I? But now I —"

"Enough chitchat, we must hurry!" the ghost **INTERRUPTED** him. "My time is ending!"

Scrooge **BLINKED**. A new place appeared before him. There, he saw a new mouse, whom he instantly recognized.

Money Is the Most Important Thing!

It was a beautiful, graceful young mouse with a **SWEET** smile.

Old Scrooge felt his heart **LEAP** as soon as he saw her. And he saw a younger version of himself as well, standing beside her. The pair was in a park, talking. It was springtime, and the *snow* had all melted.

"What's the matter, Belle?" young Scrooge asked, sounding *annoyed*.

The young mouse *bowed* her head and her chin trembled. It seemed like she was about to cry.

"Someone took my place in your **HEART**, dear Ebenezer," she replied. "Or rather, *something*."

"*Nonsense!*" the young Scrooge replied. "And what might that be, hmmm?"

Belle looked him straight in the snout. Her bright blue eyes were brimming with tears.

"Money, Ebenezer," she said softly. "It seems to be the only thing on your mind these days."

"Nonsense, nonsense!" muttered the young Scrooge. He paced back and forth **nervously**. "I'm simply trying to earn as much as possible so that I can build a life with you! Don't you understand?!"

Belle twirled her hair and shook her head sadly.

"You're the one who doesn't understand, Ebenezer," she replied. "By the time you earn enough money to make yourself truly happy, it will be too late for us. Don't you remember how happy we used to be?

When we met, we were poor, but we shared everything. We worked hard, thinking of our future. Then you asked me to marry you, and everything changed."

"We can't get married if I'm not rich!" young Scrooge **snapped** back. "I want to be able to take care of you and give you a good life! Don't you want to live in an **elegant** house, with everything you desire?"

Belle looked at him with compassion.

"Poor Ebenezer," she murmured. She took his paws and held them in her own. "Do you really think I want to be **RICH**? That money can buy happiness? You've changed, Ebenezer. You've become **greedy**. You've forgotten the most important thing."

"**Money** is the most important thing!" Scrooge burst out in exasperation. "If you

can't see that, then maybe we should part ways."

Belle brushed away a **TEAR**. There was nothing to be done. Not long ago, young Ebenezer had been a mouse who had happily **enjoyed** the same simple things she had but the desire for riches had taken over his heart.

"You're right, Ebenezer," she replied sadly. "For you, money *is* the most important thing. I wish you greater happiness with your earnings than you would have found with me. If you think of me years from now, know that I loved you very much."

The young Scrooge nodded curtly, and Belle walked away.

As old Scrooge watched the memory, he felt a sharp pang. He remembered his younger self at that time. He had pushed aside a tiny voice that told him he was letting a *precious treasure* slip away. But his greed had been stronger than his love.

"Belle," Scrooge whispered. "My dear Belle, I also loved you very much! I shouldn't have let you go."

The ghost said **NOTHING**.

Leave Me in
Peace, Ghost!

The scene changed again. Scrooge and the ghost found themselves in another place—a small room that was shabby but **FULL** of warmth.

The little stove was lit, and the fire shined on the face of a beautiful mouse.

"That's Belle!" cried old Scrooge.

But the Ghost of Christmas Past shook her head. "Look closer," she **URGED** him.

Scrooge looked again. He saw that even though the mouse **resembled** Belle, it wasn't her. In fact, Belle was sitting right beside the younger mouse! She was much **OLDER** than Scrooge remembered her, and it looked like the mouse next to her was her daughter.

The pair was surrounded by a crowd of ROWDY mouselets. The little ones ran around the room, laughing and shouting happily.

Suddenly, the door flew open, and an older mouse came in. His arms were full of packages covered in SIMPLE brown paper. They clearly weren't expensive GIFTS, but the children immediately threw themselves at the newcomer as if he were Santa Claus himself.

"Papa! Papa!" they shouted. "What did you bring us, Papa?!"

They grabbed on to his scarf, rummaged in his pockets, and tugged at his arms and legs.

"Calm down, little ones!" Belle cried, laughing. She gathered them up lovingly. "Give your papa some room to breathe!"

His fur was messy and his clothes were rumpled, but his large brown eyes SPARKLED like the sun.

When each mouselet had identified his or her own package, the mouse collapsed into a chair, exhausted. The smallest one went over and climbed into his lap, hugging him tightly.

Old Scrooge felt his heart ache. Oh, if only he had married Belle, rather than WORRYING about earning money! Then he might have been the one receiving such a sweet embrace every night!

"Enough, enough!" Scrooge shouted, pulling at his fur. "Leave me in peace, SPIRIT! Please take me away! Why do you keep reminding me that my life is so sad and lonely?"

The light emanating from the little ghost

was so intense that Scrooge squashed down the hat on her head as if to extinguish it.

Then, as quickly as she had appeared, the spirit disappeared.

Scrooge was back in his bedroom. Exhausted, he climbed into his bed and fell into a **DEEP** sleep.

Part Three

The Ghost of Christmas Present

Bong!

Scrooge sat up with a start. How long had he slept? It was **DARK**, and the bell had just struck one. But how could it be one o'clock again? Had a whole day gone by already?

Scrooge sat up in his bed and rubbed his snout with his paws. He felt confused, lost, and DEEPLY unhappy. The memory of the long journey into his own past **tormented** him. And he knew it wasn't over yet!

Marley's ghost had told Scrooge he would be visited by three spirits. That meant there were still two more to come.

Scrooge dragged himself out of bed. This time he would be ready. No ghost was going to SURPRISE him! He waited and waited while the echo of the bells faded. Five minutes passed, then ten, then fifteen. Still, nothing happened.

Scrooge sat still in his armchair, **trembling**. Then, all of a sudden, the old mouse was surrounded by a rosy **halo**. He stood up silently and followed the light. It was coming from the door to the next room.

Quietly, he shuffled over to the doorway, holding his breath.

The instant he touched the doorknob, a *deep voice* called out to him. "Enter, Scrooge!"

Scrooge obeyed immediately. He walked into his own sitting room to find it had changed: GREEN LEAVES of holly, ivy, and mistletoe hung from the ceiling. The branches were covered in sparkling red and white berries. Finally, a roaring fire raged in the fireplace.

Scrooge's eyes widened. He had never seen such a huge fire in his own home! Piled on the floor in front of the warm hearth were serving dishes full of food, grapes, juicy oranges, entire roasts, plates of pudding, and gigantic loaves of bread.

Scrooge couldn't believe his eyes. But that wasn't all! In front of the mound of food, an enormouse giant was sprawled out, a torch shaped like a cornucopia in his hand. He wore a long green robe lined with white fur and a belt with a scabbard attached, but no sword.

Instantly, Scrooge knew the **Ghost of**

86

Christmas Present was before him.

"Come forward, Scrooge!" the ghost urged him.

The old mouse took a few tentative steps forward and was bathed in light.

The Ice Melts

The giant observed Scrooge, his green **EYES** amused.

"Ha, ha, ha!" He chuckled. His huge belly jiggled. "You've never seen someone like me before, have you?"

Scrooge shook his head. At least the ghost seemed friendly.

"No, never," he confirmed, eyes wide.

"It's remarkable, isn't it?" the ghost continued with a grin. "And to think that I have more than eighteen hundred brothers!"

"That's a very **LARGE** family!" Scrooge said, shocked. Then he cleared his throat.

"Spirit, last night the Ghost of Christmas Past took me to places that reminded me of many things," Scrooge went on. "At first

I was **angry**. But I understand why she took me to see those far-off memories. So, take me wherever you wish. I'm sure you have another *lesson* to teach me."

The giant **smiled**. "Grab on to my belt," he said. "Come on, let's go!"

Scrooge obeyed. In a flash, the *holly*, ivy, berries, food, and warm fire receded. The giant and Scrooge found themselves on a city street. It was the same street the old mouse had traveled the night before on his way home from his office.

The houses were covered in a blanket of white **snow**, and the sky was heavy with clouds.

But the crowd walked along **HAPPILY**,

as if it were a beautiful sunny day. Mice smiled joyfully as they shoveled snow to clear the streets. Everyone seemed to be in a **GOOD** mood.

Scrooge hadn't noticed any of this the night before. He always walked with his head **DOWN**, hoping no one would disturb him.

A delicious smell wafted out of the rotisserie shop. Scrooge could see dining tables covered in delicious-looking food as he peered in each front window.

The giant accompanied Scrooge down a street in the poorer part of town. Every time he saw someone **SAD**, the giant raised his cornucopia and showered the mouse with light. Suddenly, Scrooge and the spirit were surrounded by smiles and happy shouts of **"Merry Christmas!"**

Scrooge was filled with a sense of joy that he couldn't explain. Just the day before he would have been so cranky at the sight of these poor mice CELEBRATING. But this evening, even he couldn't help smiling.

Old Scrooge could feel himself changing. Little by little, the ice around his heart was beginning to melt.

A Special Smile

It's hard to say if the **giant** was leading Scrooge straight to Bob Cratchit's house or if the pair ended up there by chance. The ghost passed right over the threshold and led the old mouse inside.

"Wh-Where are we?" Scrooge spluttered, looking around. "Why, this is just a shack! What could there possibly be to see here?"

The giant **WINKED**. "Just wait."

The little house was small and simple, but it was also warm and welcoming.

Bob Cratchit's wife was **stirring** a pot of soup.

"Oh, I can't wait until Bob gets home!" she murmured. "Let's hope Scrooge hasn't kept him at the office too late!"

The old man **blushed** and hid behind the ghost, as if the mouse could see him.

Mrs. Cratchit spread out the tablecloth with the help of her daughter Belinda. Meanwhile, her son Peter **PLUNGED** a fork into the dish of boiled potatoes, careful not to get himself dirty. He was wearing his father's elegant white collar for the occasion, and he didn't want to **RUIN** it.

The two youngest children, a boy and a girl, ran around tidying things up.

"Oh, heavens, if your father doesn't get here with Tim soon, everything will be **cold**!" Mrs. Cratchit sighed. "And where is Martha?"

Scrooge **scratched** his head. How many children did they have? It seemed like there were little mouselets everywhere!

Just then a *graceful* young mouse entered the house.

"Merry Christmas!" she greeted them. They all ran to embrace her.

"That's Martha, the oldest daughter," the giant whispered to Scrooge. "She works outside the city and only returns home for holidays."

"Martha, my child!" Her mother smiled as she scolded. "You're late!"

"Shhhh!" the two little boys squeaked from the front window. "Papa is coming! Run and hide, Martha! Don't let him see you!"

The young mouse stifled a giggle and ran to hide so she could SURPRISE her father.

Cratchit entered the house with a child clinging to his back. From the corner where he stood watching, Scrooge was immediately struck by the little one. He had a smile that warmed the heart.

"Where is Martha?" Bob Cratchit asked as he looked around with concern.

"Here I am!" Martha popped out from behind the door and threw herself at her father, causing him and the tiny mouse on his back to fall to the floor. Everyone BURST out laughing.

Even Scrooge couldn't keep from smiling at the image of his serious employee lying on the floor, BURIED under a mountain of mouselets.

A Big Heart

Bob Cratchit brushed himself off and stood to give a *kiss* to his wife. She hugged him warmly.

"How did things go for Tiny Tim?" she asked. "Did he do well?"

"**VERY WELL**," her husband replied, brushing himself off. "He was quiet and well behaved the whole time; he didn't disturb **ANYONE**! I'm not sure how he kept from getting bored while I ran errands. At one point, he saw a **beggar** and asked me if we could give him something.

"'My son, we have only a few shillings for ourselves,' I told him. 'But it's Christmas!' he cried."

Mrs. Cratchit smiled **SWEETLY** and

planted a kiss on the little mouse's head. "Your heart is too big, my little one!" she said tenderly. "I don't know how it fits in that little chest!"

Belinda and Peter helped their brother get settled at the table.

Scrooge observed Tim carefully. Only then did he realize that he wasn't able to move one of his legs. To stay on his feet, he had to lean on a WOODEN crutch!

After their meal, the Cratchit children ran to the kitchen to get the Christmas dessert. It was an ENORMOUSE pudding full of fresh fruit and spices. The mouselets carried it to the table in a solemn procession.

"Mmmmmm," everyone murmured, STARING longingly at the dessert.

Bob Cratchit sliced the PUDDING and passed the plates around the table.

At first, Belinda didn't touch it.

"It looks too *pretty* to eat!" she squeaked.

Peter didn't mind. He **GOBBLED** his portion up in an instant.

"Yum!" he cried, chewing an enormouse bite. "How delicious!"

Belinda smiled and finally took a taste of the magnificent dessert.

"A very merry Christmas, everyone!" Bob Cratchit cried, a **radiant** smile on his snout.

Why Are They So Happy?

Old Scrooge's feelings while he watched the family scene were strange and conflicted. On the one paw, he was **MOVED** by the happy smiles and the warmth and love that filled the room. But he was also confused. How could a family this **POOR** also be so happy? Though it was Christmas, there wasn't a single *present* under the tree. In fact, there wasn't even a **tree**! Were those children really happy anyway?

Scrooge studied the Cratchit children as if they were rare and *mysterious* creatures.

Above all, Scrooge studied Tiny Tim, with his thin little legs and **brilliant** smile. He seemed the happiest of them all!

Scrooge sighed. He had never been so content as a youngster. Instead, he had spent all his time doing schoolwork, yet he had never been satisfied. Young Scrooge had always been so afraid of disappointing his mother and father with a bad grade.

Seeing him lost in thought, the Ghost of Christmas Present gave Scrooge a nudge.

"He's a kind little mouse, isn't he?" the spirit commented.

"He seems so . . . so peaceful," Scrooge agreed. "Even though he's ill, I think."

The ghost nodded solemnly. "Yes, he's very ill."

Old Scrooge paled suddenly. He had a horrible thought.

"But he'll live, won't he?" Scrooge asked the ghost. "Is it very serious?"

The giant observed Scrooge curiously.

"Why, are you worried?" he asked. "That seems **strange**. Until now, you never cared much about anyone else."

"I'd like him to live, all the same," Scrooge replied.

The ghost shook his head sadly.

"Then I'm afraid I have some **BAD** news," the spirit said. "Tiny Tim is in great danger. If he doesn't receive the proper care, he won't make it."

"**Don't say that!**" Scrooge cried out in dismay. "And what do you mean by 'proper care'?"

"Oh, he needs a very expensive surgery," the giant replied with a sigh. "And the Cratchits certainly can't afford it."

Scrooge fell into a thoughtful silence. Bob Cratchit's lively voice interrupted his reverie.

"Let's have a toast!" he cried, raising a

glass. "As long as we're at it, and seeing as it's **CHRISTMAS**, let's also toast to Scrooge!"

The old mouse was startled.

"Well, if we must," Bob's wife replied **sharply**. "But you are too good, Bob! When I think of how that **stingy** old mouse uses you . . ."

"My love!" Bob cried, horrified. "Don't say such things, especially on Christmas!"

His wife **SHRUGGED**. "He won't even give you a day off."

Scrooge felt ashamed. It was true!

"That's not important!" replied Bob Cratchit. "That's just how he is. And he's alone, **poor** old mouse! He has no one at home to love him or take care of him."

Mrs. Cratchit's expression *softened* instantly. "You're right, my dear," she said, pressing a kiss to his snout. "We, however, are truly fortunate!"

Scrooge felt a hot **TEAR** roll down his wrinkled fur.

"It's true," he whispered as he watched the Cratchit family. "You are truly fortunate."

Cold Outside, Warm Inside

The evening passed in peace and happiness. At one point, Mrs. Cratchit mentioned old Scrooge again. The little mouselets all clutched one another in mock terror as they thought of their father's boss as a MEAN and grumpy old mouse.

But Bob Cratchit had a different opinion of Scrooge. In fact, he told his family he might ask his boss about a job for Peter.

"Perhaps then you, too, could bring home a salary!" Bob declared, beaming proudly at his son.

Peter perked up and adjusted his collar as if he were already a successful businessmouse.

Everyone laughed and teased Peter lovingly.

The Cratchits weren't elegant, and they certainly weren't RICH. Their shoes were **worn out**, and they didn't have a lot of food on the table. But they loved one another, helped one another, and were **kind** and **generous** to all those around them.

Scrooge thought of his rich, snobby clients. None of them ever gave Cratchit a second look. They would think the Cratchit family beneath them. Scrooge understood these thoughts. After all, that's what he himself used to think about poor families.

But how **WRONG** he had been! At that moment, Scrooge would have given up all the riches he had accumulated during his years of work in exchange for the **warm**, golden light that seemed to illuminate the Cratchit house from within.

"It's time to go," the Ghost of Christmas Present said quietly, startling Scrooge. "Grab on to my belt again. Our **JOURNEY** is not yet over."

Scrooge reluctantly held onto the ghost's belt and bid **FAREWELL** to the cozy Cratchit home.

A second later, he and the spirit found themselves back outside in the bitter cold. The pair flew over the city with the wind in their faces. Finally, they reached a **DARK** and desolate plain.

"Where are we?" Scrooge asked as he clung to the ghost, **trembling**.

"This is where the miners live," the giant

explained, raising his cornucopia and spilling **waves** of red light over that empty gray place.

Only then did Scrooge notice the modest cabin. Inside, by the light of a faint lantern, a family of miners was celebrating. Young and old, they were seated on the floor drinking hot tea. The oldest was singing a Christmas carol. Outside, his voice was lost in the **wailing wind**.

Scrooge asked himself how, in the middle of this desert, in the cold, the wind, and the DARKNESS, someone could find the strength to celebrate Christmas with such joy.

A Secret Light

Scrooge and the ghost stopped for just a *moment* to observe the miners. Then the giant took flight again, Scrooge still desperately hanging on to his belt.

This time they were headed for the **Sea**. In terror, the old mouse turned and saw the last bit of solid land—a strip of rocks—disappear behind them. The **WIND** whistled in his ears while the grand ocean bubbled below him.

About a mile from the shore, a lighthouse was perched dangerously on the edge of a cliff. **Seaweed** wound around the jagged rocks at its base, and seagulls swooped through the air around the solitary building.

Scrooge didn't understand. Why was the

ghost taking him to this place?

The giant pulled him up to the top of the lighthouse. Only then did the old mouse understand: even there, in the middle of the ENDLESS ocean, someone was celebrating the Christmas holiday.

Inside the lighthouse, the two guardians had lit a warm fire. Rays of light shined through tiny openings in the thick stone walls, illuminating the dark surface of the ocean all around them.

The two mice were seated at a weather-beaten old table. They clinked glasses and shook paws, wishing each other a very merry Christmas. The older mouse's fur was wrinkled and worn from so much time spent near the sea. Still, he sang a song in a voice that was as clear and strong as that of a much younger mouse.

Then the ghost took flight again over the dark water. Finally, they reached a ship.

"Huzzah! Huzzah!" shouted the sailors. "Merry Christmas and three cheers for all!"

Every single mouse on board—from the captain to the ship's youngest mouselet—had a kind word for his friends. Everyone chatted about their families, who were far away but close in their hearts.

The sailors' Christmas carols were carried into the night by the wind.

Scrooge watched the sailors with admiration.

Their eyes sparkled in the dark like burning coals, warmed by the joy of celebration. Even though they were on a ship in the middle of a rough sea, far away from their homes and loved ones, the sailors were making the best of things.

Old Scrooge thought that maybe *this* was the **secret** to being happy even in the midst of a storm: to have enough light in one's heart to shine even on the darkest night.

To Uncle Scrooge!

The wind continued to howl all around Scrooge. Suddenly, he heard the sound of laughter mixed in.

"HA, HA, HA, HA, HA!"

Scrooge was confused. Who could be laughing out here in the middle of the ocean? Only then did he realize that he and the spirit were no longer flying over the sea. They had been transported to a warm, well-lit, **comfortable** room somewhere. The Ghost of Christmas Present was seated next to Scrooge, and someone nearby was laughing joyfully.

"Ha, ha, ha! Ho, ho, ho!"

Scrooge couldn't help smiling. The laugh was warm, sincere, and friendly, and Scrooge found it to be CONTAGIOUS. There was also something very familiar about the voice. In fact, it sounded exactly like Scrooge's nephew, Fred!

And it *was* Fred. The old mouse found himself in the home of the very mouse he had treated so POORLY the morning of Christmas Eve. Fred and his family were in the middle of Christmas dinner, surrounded by guests.

"'Bah, humbug!' said Uncle Scrooge!" Fred was recounting for his family. "Ha, ha, ha!"

Scrooge furrowed his brow. His nephew was talking about him! And he wasn't being very kind.

"Well, at least he's RICH," Fred's wife observed. She was a very pretty mouse with a gentle smile.

"Oh, what does that have to do with

it?" Fred asked his wife. "Riches aren't really worth that much. For those who are already rich, it seems it's NEVER ENOUGH. Of course, Uncle Scrooge isn't a bad fellow. He's just a grumpy old fart. I find him very entertaining!"

Fred smiled, and Scrooge thought immediately of his sister, Fan, Fred's mother. This young mouse resembled her so much!

After dinner, the young mice organized a dance, and then it was time for games. The group told riddles and played charades, and Scrooge enjoyed watching them greatly. He even participated, shouting out answers even though no one could hear him, and CHUCKLING at jokes. Every time the giant suggested they leave the party, Scrooge shook his head and wrung his paws.

"Can we stay for just one more game?" he begged. "Please?"

The spirit relented and agreed. But at last the evening wound down, and Fred raised his glass in one last toast.

"To Uncle Scrooge!" he squeaked.

The old mouse's heart was lighter than it had been in a long time. But the scene suddenly vanished in the BLINK of an eye.

Farewell, Ghost!

It had been a **long** night. Scrooge and the giant traveled together to many places, witnessing scenes of joy and happiness as the spirit released waves of warm, golden light from his cornucopia. He spread hope to the **hearts** of those who were suffering or less fortunate.

Scrooge had learned to understand who needed the most **help**, and he pointed out the poorest, neediest, and most lonely souls to the ghost.

TIME flew and stood still all at once. Scrooge was bewildered by it all. How could it still be Christmas even as they moved through time?

It was like he had lived through ten, or a hundred, or a thousand Christmases all at once, condensed into a single night.

Something else strange was happening: as the night went on, the Ghost of Christmas Present was growing **OLDER**. His full cheeks grew tight, and his long red hair turned white. This change didn't escape Scrooge.

"Are you all right?" the old mouse asked the giant.

"My hour is almost up," the ghost explained, his voice tired. "At midnight, you will once again be in your bed, and I will disappear."

Scrooge grew sad.

After so many adventures together, he didn't want this warm, **happy** spirit to leave him.

"Isn't there anything you can do to stay?" Scrooge asked. "The poor need you!"

The ghost gave him a bitter smile. "Aren't there shelters for that?" he whispered. "Hospitals and nursing homes?"

Scrooge was ashamed as he remembered the words he'd said to the two kind GENTLEMICE who had come to his office earlier that evening. He looked up to ask the spirit to *forgive him*, but the ghost was gone. In his place was something else.

Part Four

The Ghost of Christmas Future

The third ghost to visit Scrooge was a dark, mysterious **shadow**. He was wearing a heavy, hooded cloak, and he approached Scrooge slowly and silently.

Scrooge took a few steps backward. After the reassuring, cheerful presence of the giant, this **GLOOMY** ghost made his fur stand on end!

The large hood **COVERED** the ghost's entire face. The only visible part of his body was a hand emerging from one sleeve of the cloak.

As the ghost approached him, Scrooge felt his **powerful** presence, and it filled him with *fear*.

"A-are you the Gh-Ghost of Christmas F-Future?" Scrooge asked timidly.

The spirit nodded but stayed silent.

Scrooge felt his knees tremble as he stood in front of the spirit, terrified. He still couldn't see the ghost's face, though it was clear to him that the spirit was observing him carefully from beneath his hood.

"O-Okay, g-guide me, sp-spirit!" Scrooge stuttered, impatient to find out what was in store for him in the future. "When I look at you, I feel frightened even though I know you are here for my own good. The two GHOSTS before you taught me many things about myself, and I know you are here to do the same."

The **ghost** stayed completely silent. After a few long moments, he stretched out his hand and motioned for the **old mouse** to follow him.

Who Would
Shed a Tear?

Scrooge followed the Ghost of Christmas Future with a mixture of FEAR and impatience. A second later, Scrooge realized they were no longer in his bedroom.

Instead, they were walking along a street. Or at least it *seemed* they were on a street. The road was so DARK and silent that it looked like a tunnel. Then, suddenly, Scrooge and the spirit were in the middle of a crowd in the center of a town square. Scrooge recognized it immediately: it was the stock exchange.

Merchant mice ran back and forth, the coins in their pockets jingling as they chattered in hurried tones. Scrooge watched as they tugged on their gold chains to check the time on their fancy watches.

If Scrooge had been able to **LOOK** each one of them in the eye, he could have said exactly what each mouse was **thinking**. He knew these mice as well as he knew himself because they were all the same. The crowd made Scrooge feel uneasy. He wasn't sure why, but he had a bad feeling.

The Ghost of Christmas Future stopped near a group of businessmice and gestured for Scrooge to approach them. Soon he was **listening** to their conversation.

"Is it true the old cranky mouse kicked the bucket?" one of them asked.

"I can't believe it!" replied another mouse.

Scrooge **JUMPED**. Had one of his clients died? But who could it be?

"Why, yes. It happened last night, on Christmas," said the first mouse.

"I thought he'd live forever with that hard shell of his!" The second mouse chuckled.

"What about all the money he made?" asked a mouse with a handlebar moustache.

"I have no idea," came the reply. "I'm sure he didn't leave it to his family, though. He was too STINGY for that!"

As they laughed, Scrooge grew more and more uneasy.

"When is the funeral?" asked a mouse who had been silent until that moment.

"I doubt anyone will attend. Why would they? Who would shed a tear over that mean, cranky old mouse?!"

Scrooge bowed his head. He wanted to ask the Ghost of Christmas Future if these mice were talking about him, but he didn't **dare**. He was TOO afraid of the answer.

A Sad, Sad Place

Scrooge looked around for himself in the crowd. On a morning like this one, he, too, would have been there in the square with the others.

He slipped away to his usual **corner**. There his clients would meet him for business. He was often there for hours and hours, STRIKING deals with one mouse after another. But there was NO ONE in his corner this morning. Scrooge started to get a bad feeling in the pit of his stomach.

Maybe he got held up at the office! Or perhaps he wasn't feeling well this morning. How far in the future had they traveled anyway? He had a million questions he was much to afraid to ask.

A Sad, Sad Place

The Ghost of Christmas Future stayed **BESIDE** Scrooge, silent. Deep in thought and with a heavy heart, Scrooge left the LIVELY town square and soon found himself in a neighborhood he had never been to before.

The streets were dirty and narrow, the stores and houses were shabby, and the mice were wearing rags. Groups of mice were seated on the sidewalk even though it was covered in dirt.

Scrooge walked slowly past these poor beggars. He wished there was something he could do to help them. But he wasn't even sure he could help himself at the moment. Finally, at the end of a long, dark maze of buildings, the old mouse and the ghost reached a shop.

The shelves were cluttered with rusted

keys, scraps of metal, rags, and dusty bottles of all SHAPES and sizes. An elderly mouse with stringy, **prickly** white fur and small, *shrewd* eyes sat on a box in the middle of the stall. Scrooge had never seen him before.

We'll Divide Up the Loot!

While Scrooge observed the mouse on the box, another mouse dressed in rags entered the little stall. She put her HEAVY bundle down on the ground. Soon another mouse joined her. She, too, had a HEAVY bundle. Finally, a mouse dressed all in black entered.

The four mice looked at one another and suddenly they all burst out laughing.

"You're here, too?" the old mouse asked the newcomer dressed in black. "A washermouse, a servant, and an undertaker. My word, what a group!"

The three mice shared an awkward look.

"Well, I think we're all here for the same reason, aren't we?" the washermouse guessed.

"Certainly," the old mouse confirmed. Then he lit a candle and looked at the others craftily. "Let's see what you each managed to steal, and then we'll divide up the LOOT. If we wait much longer, we may be DISCOVERED."

The others quickly opened the bundles they had brought with them.

"I have an **OLD** pin, a pair of cuff links, two coats, and two teaspoons," said the first mouse.

"I found much less," the undertaker said. "The only thing I managed to grab was a pair of **patent leather** shoes."

"What do you say to these?" the servant asked as she pulled out two large, *patterned* bed curtains.

The other mice gasped.

"That's a real treasure, my friend!" the washermouse congratulated her.

"Isn't it?" the servant **gloated** proudly. "After all, they're no longer any good to *him*."

Scrooge stared at the curtains, and his breath caught in his THROAT. Those belonged to him! And the teaspoons, the coats, the shoes, and the cuff links — those were his, too! These scoundrels had ransacked *his house*!

Take Me Away, Spirit!

But the worst was still to come.

"I have one more thing of great value," the washermouse said. "I've kept it **hidden**, but we can also share the profits from selling this."

With that she *PULLED* a white shirt out from her bundle. It was very well made.

"It's the BEST one he owned!" the mouse said proudly. "Look here: it's made of white cotton, with mother-of-pearl buttons He was wearing it when he **DIED**, but I managed to get it off him. He was all alone, so it was easy! No mouse needs such an *elegant* shirt on the other side. And no one will be at his **funeral**, so who will even know?"

"Well said!" The old scoundrel chuckled with great SATISFACTION.

It was too much! Scrooge stared at his shirt, horrified. He had to get out of there immediately! Scrooge grabbed the Ghost of Christmas Future by the cloak and shook him. But the ghost didn't move an inch.

"Spirit, spirit!" the old mouse cried, his whiskers *trembling*. "I understand! I know what you're trying to tell me. I know exactly who the cranky old mouse is. It's me! It's me! I've learned my lesson, **I promise**! Take me away now, please. I beg you! I don't want to be in this time any longer!"

Without a **WORD**, the ghost slowly retraced their path, leading Scrooge away

from the dingy stall. Scrooge followed him **nervously**, looking around in fear of seeing other beggars along the way dividing up objects they'd stolen from him.

Then, suddenly, he tripped. Scrooge felt himself falling into a large, **DEEP** hole.

With a start, Scrooge found himself in an entirely new place. It was a cold, empty room with a cast-iron bed right in the middle. A faint light filtered in through the window and illuminated the mattress, where there was someone laid out beneath a sheet.

There was no one else in the room. Scrooge had no way of knowing if the mouse in the bed was still alive or not, but he had a bad feeling in his stomach.

The Ghost of Christmas Future gestured

toward the bed. Scrooge SHOOK his head fearfully and backed away.

"No, no," he WHISPERED. His fur was as white as a slice of mozzarella. "Whoever this mouse is, seeing him here **alone** and abandoned has broken my heart. What did he do in life to deserve such loneliness? Was he greedy and selfish? Did he think only of himself, without ever helping his friends and family during times of need? If so, whoever he is, he is just like me!"

Shaken, Scrooge knelt down at the foot of the bed and sobbed.

He cried not just for this mouse, but also for himself. Surely this was the future that awaited him as punishment for a life of greed and insensitivity.

But just then Scrooge had a

GLIMMER of hope. He knew the PAST could not change, but maybe be had a chance to change the future. Was it too late for him? Scrooge hoped not.

Good News or Bad?

Scrooge turned to the ghost to make a request.

"Please," he said, "show me if there's someone, even a single mouse in the entire city, who is CRYING over the loss of this poor creature."

The ghost spread out his dark cloak like a pair of wings in front of him. Then he lowered his arms and Scrooge's surroundings changed yet again. The cast-iron bed faded away. In its place, a mother and her children APPEARED.

She was pacing back and forth anxiously, tHROWiNG constant looks at the clock and peering out the window.

Finally, the front door opened, and her

husband entered. The mouse rushed to greet him and held him tightly. But then she saw his expression, and she stepped back, **worried**.

"Is it bad news?" she asked, concerned.

Her husband sighed. "I'm afraid it's the worst news for one mouse, my dear wife. But at the same time, it is good news for us."

The children scurried over, trying to grasp what was happening.

"I don't understand," the mouse said. "Whatever do you mean, my dear?"

"I'm afraid our old creditor is **DEAD**," explained her husband. "Though I'm sad to say it, this is good news for us."

The mouse was a merchant who had **BORROWED** money from a creditor a long time ago. Unfortunately, he had never managed to pay off his debt.

"But that means there's still hope!" cried the wife, her face lighting up.

Her husband nodded. "Yes," he agreed. "Our debt has not been paid, but the old creditor didn't make a plan for a will before he died. Eventually, I'm sure the debt will pass on to another businessmouse. But in the meantime, we will be able to scrape together what we will need in order to finally PAY OFF our loan."

"Then we're saved!" the mother mouse cried happily. Her relief was so great that she burst into tears.

In the corner where he stood witnessing this scene, Scrooge bowed his head.

"I understand, spirit," he said sadly. "That man in the cast-iron bed was a creditor. And the only mouse in the city who is crying over his loss is crying tears of joy!"

Scrooge sighed. "Well, spirit, I hope you will do one more thing for me. Show me someone who is surrounded by love and affection?"

The Ghost of Christmas Future *slipped* quietly out of the room. Scrooge found himself faced with a now-familiar front door. The PLAQUE overhead read:

The Cratchits

Like a Little Bird

Scrooge felt his heart leap. The memory of the warmth and HAPPINESS of the Cratchit household comforted him after so many sad and depressing scenes.

Inside, Mrs. Cratchit was seated at the table in front of the fireplace, surrounded by her children.

The two youngest were *cuddled* up and listening to Peter. The boy was no longer wearing his father's collar. Instead he had a book open on his knees, and he was reading ALOUD.

Belinda was sewing beside her mother. Martha, the oldest, was not home.

Scrooge searched the room for signs of Tiny Tim, but he didn't see him. As he looked more closely at the Cratchits, Scrooge realized something was off. The entire family seemed strangely still compared to the last time, when he had seen them celebrating Christmas so JOYFULLY.

"When is Papa getting home?" Peter asked, interrupting his reading.

As if on command, the front door jiggled and flew open.

"Papa!" squealed the two little Cratchits, jumping to greet him. "It took you so long to come back!"

Scrooge smiled tenderly. At last, he was watching a heartwarming scene like the ones he had enjoyed so much the night before!

"It takes me a bit longer because I'm getting older," Bob Cratchit replied, patting his children affectionately.

"And to think that once you flew down the

streets as quick as lightning, even with Tiny Tim on your shoulders!" his wife recalled, holding Bob's paws in her own.

Scrooge was startled. If Tiny Tim didn't need to be carried anymore, maybe it was because he had been HEALED!

This cheered the old mouse up as he watched Bob Cratchit embrace his wife tenderly.

"You're right, my dear," Cratchit said softly. "Our Tiny Tim weighed so little. He was like a little bird!"

Scrooge flinched, as if he had picked a *beautiful* rose and suddenly been pricked by a thorn.

Weighed? Scrooge thought. Why was he speaking in the PAST tense?

"You know, I ran into Scrooge's nephew, Fred," Cratchit told his wife. "He was very KIND, and he seemed upset to hear about Tiny Tim."

"What a dear one he is," Mrs. Cratchit replied, touched.

Then it was true: Tiny Tim had passed away and was gone from this earth forever. Scrooge felt as though his heart had been crushed into a million pieces.

It's Not Too Late!

Scrooge realized that none of the future Christmases he had seen had been in order. They had been skipping around in time. He felt **tiReD**, sad, and **CONFUSED**.

"Please, spirit," he requested. "Take me to my house. Show me what will happen to me on a **future** Christmas."

He quietly followed the ghost down the road that led to the office of Scrooge and Marley.

Scrooge stood at the front window and **PEERED** inside: the office was open, even on Christmas. The walls had been freshly painted and a mouse Scrooge had never seen before was seated at his desk.

"Who is that?" Scrooge asked the spirit.

But the ghost did not reply. Instead, he led Scrooge **away** from the office and down another street. Scrooge followed as they crossed the city and ended up in front of his house.

"This is my house," Scrooge said. "I know this is the place."

He stopped to look at the front door he knew So weLL. This was the very door knocker that had changed into the snout of Jacob Marley's ghost just the night before.

But the ghost did not stop. Instead, he continued to lead Scrooge across that street, and then across another.

"But where are you taking me?" Scrooge asked, hurrying to **KEEP UP**. "My house was back there!"

Finally, they arrived at the local CEMETERY.

"But why did you bring me here?!" Scrooge

asked, appalled. "You don't mean to say that . . ."

As usual, the spirit remained silent. The cloaked figure simply led Scrooge to a headstone that STOOD OUT from the others.

Scrooge approached it cautiously. As soon as he saw the inscription, he shivered. The name carved on the stone was:

Ebenezer Scrooge

The old mouse turned as WHITE as a slice of mozzarella.

"Spirit, please tell me one thing," he whispered. "Will what I'm seeing now surely come to pass, or is this what *could* happen?"

The ghost did not reply.

"I can change!" Scrooge shouted. "No, I *want* to change! I've learned so many things these past few nights, and now I know that

I **must** change! Oh, spirit, I beg you. Please tell me there's still a **chance** for me!"

The Ghost of Christmas Future remained silent. It wasn't up to him to decide the **FATE** of this mouse. Scrooge himself had to change his own fate.

"Please!" Scrooge continued, grabbing the ghostly hand that hung from the bottom of the spirit's cloak. "I am not the mouse I was. I have relived my past, and I know now that I was **wrong**. Oh, I was a fool in so many ways! Oh, please, spirit, listen to me! I am truly sorry. I want to **change**!"

He grabbed on to the ghost's cloak, as if he wanted to keep him there. But the ghost remained **STILL** and **silent**.

"Doesn't every **mouse** have the right to a second chance?" Scrooge begged.

"I know I'm old, and I've made many **mistakes**, but I still have time to fix them. Please tell me it isn't too late to change my life!"

The ghost wriggled out of Scrooge's grasp. Scrooge lifted his eyes up just in time to see the ghost's hood and cloak shrink and **TRANSFORM** into a bedpost.

Part Five

What a Marvemouse Day!

Scrooge closed his eyes and then opened them again. Was he really back in his own bedroom, in his own home? Had it all been just a *dream*?

Where was the CEMETERY? Where was the Ghost of Christmas Future, who had been beside him just a moment earlier? Why, the ghost must have heard his request and granted it. He was getting his second chance after all!

Scrooge was more EXCITED than he had been in ages, and he was full of good intentions. He leaped out of bed and saw that the curtains were still hanging there. NO ONE had stolen them!

He jumped for joy and hugged the curtains as if they were **dear** friends. Then Scrooge raced to his closet and quickly got dressed. He wanted to do so many things!

"What kind of day will today be?" he asked himself. For the first time in his life, Scrooge realized he had NO IDEA! He felt like a child who barely knew his own name. And yet he couldn't wait to get out in the **WORLD** and see what awaited him there.

He ran to his window and threw it open. The air was cold and brisk, and Scrooge breathed it in deeply. The sun was shining down on London, making the snow on the roofs *sparkle* and **shine**. The previous night's fog had lifted, and there wasn't a single cloud in the sky. It was a splendid day!

The bells were ringing merrily: DING, DONG, DING, DONG...

What an enchanting sound! Scrooge **leaned** out the window and spied a young mouselet walking along the street.

"What day is it today?" he asked.

"Why, don't you know?!" the little mouse replied, surprised. "It's **Christmas**, sir!"

Scrooge lit up.

Christmas!

To his great **SURPRISE**, Scrooge realized his journeys with the three ghosts had occurred in a single night. Barely any time had passed, and he was just in time to celebrate the holiday!

"How wonderful!" he cried, clapping his paws with happiness. "That's **fantastic**!"

The mouse looked up at him, confused. Scrooge winked.

"Listen, do you know the

meat shop down the street?" Scrooge asked.

The little mouse nodded.

"Have they sold that enormouse turkey that's been on display in the window?"

The mouse scratched his head. "No, no, they certainly haven't sold it," he replied. "It's **very expensive**!"

"Oh, good!" cheered Scrooge.

The mouselet held back a giggle. What a strange old rodent!

"Please, run and buy it for me," Scrooge asked politely. Then he tossed a bag of gold pieces to the mouse.

The mouselet scampered off like a flash of lightning.

"I'll send it to the Cratchits!" Scrooge said, RUBBING his paws together happily. Poor Cratchit was such a hard worker! He was never late, he never COMPLAINED, and

he never asked for a raise even though his family was so poor! Oh, dear, dear Cratchit!

Scrooge couldn't wait to see his employee and meet his adorable little mouselets, especially TINY TIM!

In the EXCiTEMENT of the moment, he put his pants on inside out, his socks were mismatched, and his hat was askew. When  he looked in the mirror, he burst out LAUGHiNG. Oh, how wonderful it was to laugh! He hadn't done it in so long, he hardly recognized the sound.

Scrooge tidied himself up and finally left the house. On his way out the door, he met the mouselet as he RETURNED with the huge turkey. Scrooge gave the little mouse the piece of paper with the Cratchits' address and gave him a big tip.

The mouselet was confused as he looked up at Scrooge and thanked him *sincerely*. Then he took the money and rushed off to deliver the gift to the Cratchits. He had never seen any mouse do anything so **generous** in his whole life!

Scrooge watched as the little mouselet scampered off, an **ENORMOUSE** grin on his snout. His smile grew even **LARGER** as he gave a sack of coins to a beggar. Scrooge continued to smile happily as he scampered down the street.

For perhaps the first time in his life, Ebenezer Scrooge was so happy he felt he might **BURST**!

Scrooge's Transformation

Scrooge walked down the street, his paws behind his back as though he didn't have a care in the world. There was a merry smile on his snout, and he seemed so *happy* that mice passing by couldn't help themselves from *greeting* him and wishing him well.

"Good day, sir!" they said warmly. "Merry Christmas!"

Those were some of the most wonderful words Scrooge had ever heard.

He hadn't been walking for too long before he ran into one of the two GENTLEMICE who had visited him on Christmas Eve to ask for donations.

Scrooge's heart ached thinking back on how he had treated the two mice so poorly.

"My friend!" Scrooge cried, *RUSHING* over to the mouse. "How are you? Did you and your companion manage to gather enough donations?"

The gentlemouse **STARED** at Scrooge as if he had never seen him before in his life.

"Mr. . . . Mr. Scrooge?" he **stuttered**, his eyes wide with surprise.

"Yes, it's me!" Scrooge confirmed, chuckling. Then his snout grew **serious**. "Forgive me. Who knows what you must have thought of me yesterday. I know I do not have a good *reputation*."

The gentlemouse blushed. He had no idea how to respond. In fact, he and his partner had never been treated so **rudely** in their entire career!

"Oh, but now everything has changed!" Scrooge rushed to add. "And I want to contribute to your good works. Here, allow me to give you a small donation right away."

Scrooge placed a sack of jingling coins in the gentlemouse's paws. The mouse was so surprised he was **afraid** to take the money.

"Are you serious?!" he asked. Then he saw how eagerly Scrooge was nodding. He shrugged and accepted the gift **gratefully**. "I don't know what to say!"

"Don't say anything!" Scrooge replied with great **satisfaction**. "I've added extra to make up for all the money I should have donated in years past. Will you please promise to come ask me again next year?"

The gentlemouse promised, and Scrooge

left him in the middle of the street, the *generous* donation in his paw. The poor mouse had the expression of someone who had just seen a **ghost**!

Are You Feeling All Right, Uncle?

After watching his nephew's Christmas party the previous **NIGHT**, Scrooge couldn't wait to see Fred again. He wanted to wrap him up in a big hug and ask for his **forgiveness** for the unkind way Scrooge had treated him on Christmas Eve morning. And much of his life before that!

When he reached his nephew's house, Scrooge must have walked up to the **front door** at least a dozen times before he finally got up the courage to knock.

Knock, knock, knock!

A strange mouse opened the door. "Yes?"

"Hello, is Fred at home?" Scrooge asked, peering through the doorway. He saw his

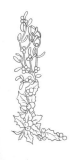

nephew in the sitting room and ran to embrace him.

Fred was **squeakless**.

"U-Uncle!" he stammered. "Are you feeling all right?"

"Oh, I'm **wonderful**!" Scrooge replied. "I'm just wonderful! Merry Christmas, my dear nephew!"

Fred's wife watched the scene before her in **surprise**. This would be a truly memorable Christmas!

Once he was sure his uncle was truly all right and hadn't lost his senses, Fred greeted him warmly. He was so happy to have Scrooge there to celebrate the holiday. At last, the family was reunited!

Fred invited Scrooge to stay for lunch, and Scrooge accepted gladly. Together, the family ate, **SANG** carols, and played

games. Scrooge made many toasts and enjoyed himself as he never had before.

When the night was over, Scrooge felt happier than he had ever been. He said good-bye to his family and thanked them warmly.

"You are all truly wonderful," he complimented them. "Promise to come visit me soon!"

When he finally left them, they waved good-bye, smiling but still feeling a bit confused, as if they had witnessed something truly EXTRAORDINARY.

Can I Call You Bob?

he next morning, Scrooge **woke up** early. He wanted to arrive in the office before Bob Cratchit. Scrooge settled in at his desk and waited for Cratchit.

The office clock had just **struck** nine on the dot when poor Bob arrived, out of breath.

When he saw that his boss was already there, his snout fell. He immediately prepared for Scrooge to dock his pay since he had been **late to work**.

"I-I'm sorry, sir!" he panted. "We celebrated until very **LATE** last night."

Scrooge had carefully prepared what he was going to say and kept a **serious** look on his snout. He looked at Cratchit sternly.

"Yes," Scrooge observed. "It seems to me you're a bit **LATE** this morning."

Poor Bob bowed his head.

"I am truly sorry, sir," he replied. "I promise it will never happen again!"

At that point, Scrooge couldn't contain himself any longer. He **LEAPED** off the stool and shook Bob Cratchit's paw **warmly**.

"Come now, it's nothing serious!" Scrooge reassured him, smiling. "And I have some good news: since it's Christmas, I've decided to **DOUBLE** your salary!"

Bob Cratchit stared at Scrooge as if he'd lost his fur.

"Are . . . are you joking, sir?" he asked in shock. Bob Cratchit didn't know what to think. He had never known Scrooge to joke about something as **serious** as money.

In fact, he had never known Scrooge to joke about anything at all!

"I'm serious!" Scrooge replied. "You're an excellent worker, Cratchit, and you and your **lovely** family deserve it."

Bob scratched his head, confused. "B-But, I don't believe you've ever even met my family."

"Oh, that doesn't matter," Scrooge rushed to say. "I've heard great things about them! So, from now on your salary is doubled. And no complaining, eh?! Merry Christmas, my dear Bob."

Scrooge clapped a friendly paw on his employee's shoulder.

"Can I call you Bob?" he asked.

Bob Cratchit couldn't believe his ears.

He stood there squeakless, STARING at the old mouse.

"Oh, of c-course, sir," he stammered, still in **shock**. "I mean, you can call me whatever you want."

"Good," Scrooge said. "We'll discuss your **PAY** and a few other small things at lunch, then. But for now, just know that I want to help you, my dear Bob, as you have always helped me. This whole business would go under without you!"

Cratchit blushed, both embarrassed and happy. It was as if he were *dreaming*!

"And that's not all," Scrooge added, a huge smile spreading across his snout. "I know that your ***youngest*** son is so ill he cannot walk.

"Your Tiny Tim is a good **CHILD**, and I want him to have a long life so he can bring

JOY to us all. I will pay all the medical bills. Don't worry about a thing. From now on, Bob Cratchit, things will be better!"

The clerk shook his head in **disbelief**. He didn't know what to think! Confused and touched, he could do nothing but **HUG** the old mouse.

Merry Christmas to All!

Scrooge was a mouse of his **word**. From that day forward, he took care of the Cratchits as if they were his own family. And he also took care of many others.

And that's not all! He became the best **friend**, the best **BOSS**, and the best **CITIZEN**, but not just right there in London. Scrooge did whatever he could to help mice in cities all over England!

Many of the mice who knew Scrooge laughed at this change. The merchants who were used to seeing him so ill-tempered, bitter, and difficult joked with him and scolded him for turning into such a **soft** mouse.

But Scrooge didn't care. He knew they were just **JEALOUS** of his happiness. Plus, Scrooge had learned that there were many things more important than the reputation of a **cranky** old mouse! So those old grouches could go ahead and laugh at him! In the end, Scrooge had discovered that a good laugh was good for everymouse.

In fact, more had changed than just Scrooge's personality: his appearance had been transformed as well. The new Scrooge was truly unrecognizable: His *prickly* beard had grown long and soft like the beard of a lovable old grandfather. Scrooge's sharp features had softened, and his once-angry eyes **SPARKLED** with a **secret** light.

It was as if Scrooge had an endless supply of jokes in mind, and he was about to tell one after the next. No *ghost* ever

visited Ebenezer Scrooge again. The reason was simple: old Scrooge had learned his **LESSON**.

Tiny Tim Cratchit began to **LOVINGLY** call him "uncle." And thanks to Scrooge's generosity, Tiny Tim received the best medical care. He grew to be a **STRONG** and happy young mouse.

Naturally, Scrooge also took great care of his nephew's family. He **shared** his many savings with them so that Fred and his family no longer felt they were poor.

Finally, Scrooge took care of his neighbors, whom he had ignored for so many years. From that **moment** on, he gave out gifts, food, and shelter to those in need every Christmas.

And he didn't stop there: Scrooge was generous with

his time and money **all year round**! Thanks to the ghosts of Christmases past, present, and future, Ebenezer Scrooge had discovered that everymouse—no matter how big or small, rich or poor, kind or ill-tempered—had the right to be happy and loved.

And that, my dear readers, is where we leave this story. As Ebenezer Scrooge would say, a **warm** and **bright** merry Christmas to all!

Charles Dickens

Charles Dickens was born in Portsmouth, England, on February 7, 1812. He was a happy child who enjoyed reading. When he was ten years old, his family was forced to move to London. There, his father was arrested in 1824 because of unpaid debts. Young Charles had to help his family by working in a shoe polish factory, where he glued on labels.

When he left school several years later, Charles became a journalist and began to dedicate his life to writing.

In 1836, he published his first novel, *The Pickwick Papers*, serially in a newspaper. The work's immediate success launched Dickens into the world of English literary fame. That same year, he married Catherine Hogarth, daughter of the editor-in-chief. They had ten children together.

In 1837, Dickens published *Oliver Twist*. He then went on to write a number of other masterpieces, among them *Nicholas Nickleby* (1838), *David Copperfield* (1849), *Bleak House* (1852), *A Tale of Two Cities* (1859), and *Great Expectations* (1860). Dickens was known as an author who paid attention to the ordinary lives of people, but with great humor and wit. He is considered one of the greatest writers of all time. Charles Dickens died in 1870 at the age of fifty-eight. He is buried at Westminster Abbey.

Don't miss a single fabumouse adventure!

#1 Lost Treasure of the Emerald Eye

#2 The Curse of the Cheese Pyramid

#3 Cat and Mouse in a Haunted House

#4 I'm Too Fond of My Fur!

#5 Four Mice Deep in the Jungle

#6 Paws Off, Cheddarface!

#7 Red Pizzas for a Blue Count

#8 Attack of the Bandit Cats

#9 A Fabumouse Vacation for Geronimo

#10 All Because of a Cup of Coffee

#11 It's Halloween, You 'Fraidy Mouse!

#12 Merry Christmas, Geronimo!

#13 The Phantom of the Subway

#14 The Temple of the Ruby of Fire

#15 The Mona Mousa Code

#16 A Cheese-Colored Camper

#17 Watch Your Whiskers, Stilton!

#18 Shipwreck on the Pirate Islands

#19 My Name Is Stilton, Geronimo Stilton

#20 Surf's Up, Geronimo!

#21 The Wild, Wild West

#22 The Secret of Cacklefur Castle

A Christmas Tale

#23 Valentine's Day Disaster

#24 Field Trip to Niagara Falls

#25 The Search for Sunken Treasure

#26 The Mummy with No Name

#27 The Christmas Toy Factory

#28 Wedding Crasher

#29 Down and Out Down Under

#30 The Mouse Island Marathon

#31 The Mysterious Cheese Thief

Christmas Catastrophe

#32 Valley of the Giant Skeletons

#33 Geronimo and the Gold Medal Mystery

#34 Geronimo Stilton, Secret Agent

#35 A Very Merry Christmas

#36 Geronimo's Valentine

#37 The Race Across America

#38 A Fabumouse School Adventure

#39 Singing Sensation

#40 The Karate Mouse

#41 Mighty Mount Kilimanjaro

#42 The Peculiar Pumpkin Thief

#43 I'm Not a Supermouse!

#44 The Giant Diamond Robbery

#45 Save the White Whale!

#46 The Haunted Castle

#47 Run for the Hills, Geronimo!

#48 The Mystery in Venice

#49 The Way of the Samurai

#50 This Hotel Is Haunted!

#51 The Enormouse Pearl Heist

#52 Mouse in Space!

#53 Rumble in the Jungle

#54 Get into Gear, Stilton!

#55 The Golden Statue Plot

#56 Flight of the Red Bandit

#57 The Stinky Cheese Vacation

#58 The Super Chef Contest

#59 Welcome to Moldy Manor

#60 The Treasure of Easter Island

#61 Mouse House Hunter

#62 Mouse Overboard!

#63 The Cheese Experiment

#64 Magical Mission

#65 Bollywood Burglary

#66 Operation: Secret Recipe

#67 The Chocolate Chase

#68 Cyber-Thief Showdown

#69 Hug a Tree, Geronimo

#70 The Phantom Bandit

#71 Geronimo on Ice!

#72 The Hawaiian Heist

#73 The Missing Movie

Up Next:

Don't miss any of my adventures in the Kingdom of Fantasy!

THE KINGDOM OF FANTASY

THE QUEST FOR PARADISE:
THE RETURN TO THE KINGDOM OF FANTASY

THE AMAZING VOYAGE:
THE THIRD ADVENTURE IN THE KINGDOM OF FANTASY

THE DRAGON PROPHECY:
THE FOURTH ADVENTURE IN THE KINGDOM OF FANTASY

THE VOLCANO OF FIRE:
THE FIFTH ADVENTURE IN THE KINGDOM OF FANTASY

THE SEARCH FOR TREASURE:
THE SIXTH ADVENTURE IN THE KINGDOM OF FANTASY

THE ENCHANTED CHARMS:
THE SEVENTH ADVENTURE IN THE KINGDOM OF FANTASY

THE PHOENIX OF DESTINY:
AN EPIC KINGDOM OF FANTASY ADVENTURE

THE HOUR OF MAGIC:
THE EIGHTH ADVENTURE IN THE KINGDOM OF FANTASY

THE WIZARD'S WAND:
THE NINTH ADVENTURE IN THE KINGDOM OF FANTASY

THE SHIP OF SECRETS:
THE TENTH ADVENTURE IN THE KINGDOM OF FANTASY

THE DRAGON OF FORTUNE:
AN EPIC KINGDOM OF FANTASY ADVENTURE

THE GUARDIAN OF THE REALM:
THE ELEVENTH ADVENTURE IN THE KINGDOM OF FANTASY

THE ISLAND OF DRAGONS:
THE TWELFTH ADVENTURE IN THE KINGDOM OF FANTASY

Visit Geronimo in every universe!

Spacemice

Geronimo Stiltonix and his crew are out of this world!

Cavemice

Geronimo Stiltonoot, an ancient ancestor, is friends with the dinosaurs in the Stone Age!

Micekings

Geronimo Stiltonord lives amongst the dragons in the ancient far north!

Don't miss any of these exciting Thea Sisters adventures!

 **Thea Stilton and the Dragon's Code**

 **Thea Stilton and the Mountain of Fire**

 **Thea Stilton and the Ghost of the Shipwreck**

 **Thea Stilton and the Secret City**

 **Thea Stilton and the Mystery in Paris**

 **Thea Stilton and the Cherry Blossom Adventure**

 **Thea Stilton and the Star Castaways**

 **Thea Stilton: Big Trouble in the Big Apple**

 **Thea Stilton and the Ice Treasure**

 **Thea Stilton and the Secret of the Old Castle**

 **Thea Stilton and the Blue Scarab Hunt**

 **Thea Stilton and the Prince's Emerald**

 **Thea Stilton and the Mystery on the Orient Express**

 **Thea Stilton and the Dancing Shadows**

 **Thea Stilton and the Legend of the Fire Flowers**

 **Thea Stilton and the Spanish Dance Mission**

 **Thea Stilton and the Journey to the Lion's Den**

 **Thea Stilton and the Great Tulip Heist**

 **Thea Stilton and the Chocolate Sabotage**

 **Thea Stilton and the Missing Myth**

**Thea Stilton and the
Lost Letters**

**Thea Stilton and the
Tropical Treasure**

**Thea Stilton and the
Hollywood Hoax**

**Thea Stilton and the
Madagascar Madness**

**Thea Stilton and the
Frozen Fiasco**

**Thea Stilton and the
Venice Masquerade**

**Thea Stilton and the
Niagara Splash**

**Thea Stilton and the
Riddle of the Ruins**

**Thea Stilton and the
Phantom of the Orchestra**

**Thea Stilton and the
Black Forest Burglary**

And check out my
fabumouse special editions!

THE JOURNEY
TO ATLANTIS

THE SECRET OF
THE FAIRIES

THE SECRET OF
THE SNOW

THE CLOUD
CASTLE

THE TREASURE
OF THE SEA

THE LAND OF
FLOWERS

THE SECRET OF
THE CRYSTAL
FAIRIES

THE DANCE OF
THE STAR FAIRIES

Dear mouse friends,
Thanks for reading, and farewell
till the next book.
It'll be another whisker-licking-good
adventure, and that's a promise!

Geronimo Stilton